1 Big Salad

by
Juana Medina

Viking

1

one
Avocado Deer

2

two

Radish Mice

3

three

pepper Monkeys

4

four

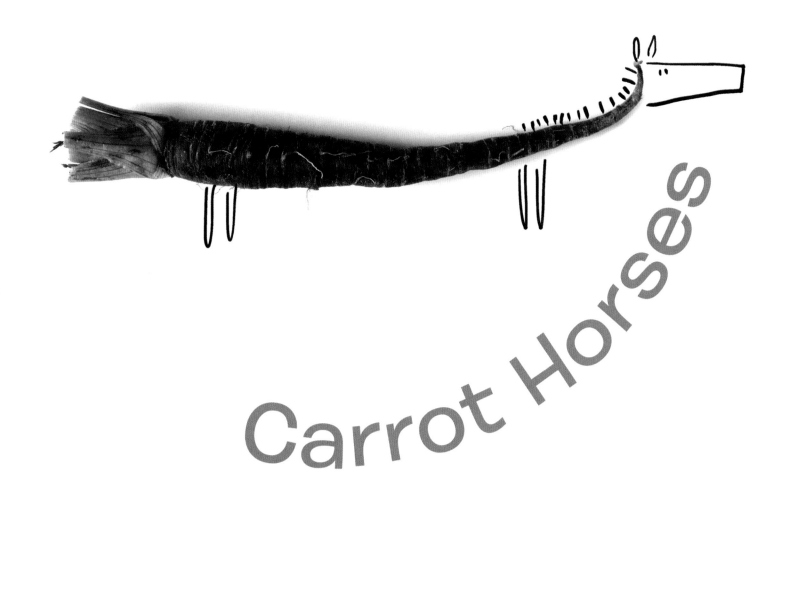

Carrot Horses

5

five

Tomato Turtles

6

six

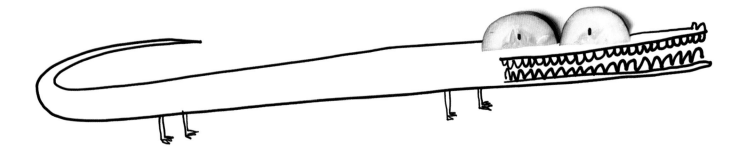

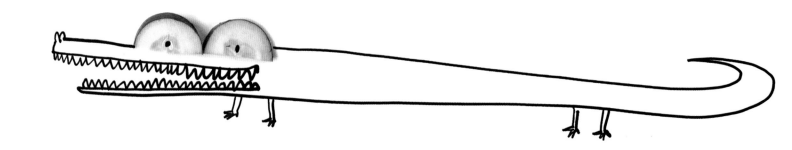

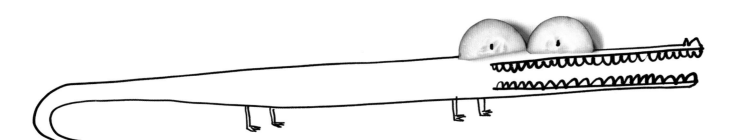

Cucumber Alligators

7

seven

8

eight

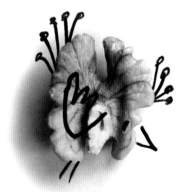

Flying Walnuts

9
nine

Romaine Dogs

10

ten

Clementine Kitties

One big delicious salad!

To Sally, for all the countless and delicious salads shared.

Viking

Penguin Young Readers Group

An imprint of Penguin Random House LLC

375 Hudson Street

New York, New York 10014

First published in the United States of America by Viking,

an imprint of Penguin Random House LLC, 2016

Copyright © 2016 by Juana Medina

LIBRARY OF CONGRESS CATALOGING-IN-PUBLICATION DATA IS AVAILABLE.

ISBN: 978-1-101-99974-5

1   3   5   7   9   10   8   6   4   2

Manufactured in China   Book design by Nancy Brennan   Set in Bodoni Six and Burbank big wide

The art for this book was created digitally, in combination with fresh fruits and vegetables from
the University of the District of Columbia (UDC) Farmers Market.

Dressing

1 teaspoon of sea salt

1/2 cup of olive oil

1/2 cup of lemon juice

A pinch of black pepper

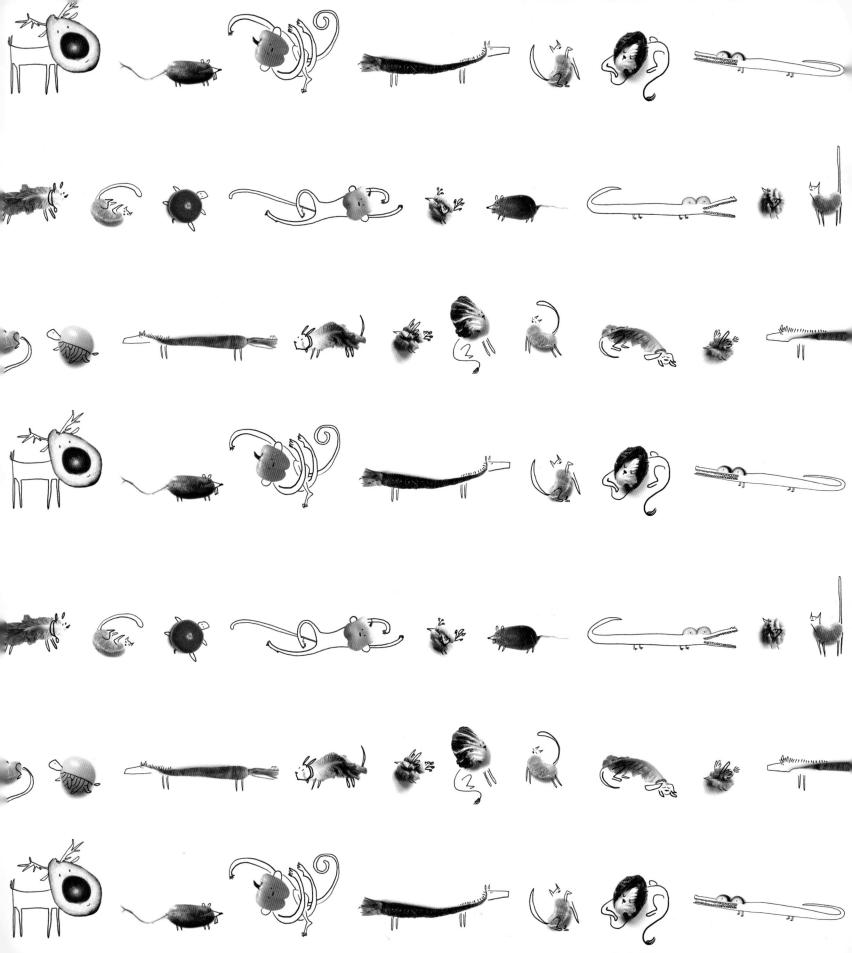